E
SPARRO
COUCH

Sparrow, Kerry Lyn

The Couch Potato

DISCARDED
Huron Public Library

W9-CVA-297

Ingram #17 10/19

THE Couch Potato

Kerry Lyn Sparrow • Yinfan Huang

Kids Can Press

HURON PUBLIC LIBRARY
521 DAKOTA AVE S
HURON, SD 57350-2797

SCHOOL BUS

It didn't belong there. No one knew where it came from. But there it was.

Mr. Russet was the first to spot it. He had just finished zipping Reid's and Violet's backpacks for school, and waving goodbye to Mrs. Russet as she headed off to work when it caught his eye. Right in the middle of the couch. A potato.

Mr. Russet had planned to do a bit of tidying in the living room, but the sight of the potato changed his mind.

"Every day I pick up this, I pick up that, I pick up everything!" he exclaimed. "I will not pick up that potato!" And he left the room without picking up anything at all.

Reid came across the potato when he got home
from school, but he didn't see a potato — he saw a
giant boulder in the middle of a farmer's field. His toy
tractors had to work together to move it. Eventually,
a mudslide buried the potato boulder.

Mrs. Russet got home from work and put her feet up to read the newspaper, but she just couldn't get comfortable. Had the couch always been this lumpy? She reached under the cushion and pulled out the potato, which she assumed was a ball, and tossed it across the room.

Frisky, the family dog, caught the potato and spent a happy hour playing with it before returning it to its spot on the couch, slightly more slobbery than it had been before.

Sometime later, Violet wandered into the room and spotted the couch potato. It looked pretty ugly just sitting there. So she dressed it in her doll's pink tutu and a baseball cap.

Mr. Russet saw the fully dressed potato sitting on the couch and blinked. It was a vegetable, for goodness' sake, not a houseguest!

His fingers twitched and he nearly picked it up, but instead he shoved his hands deep into his pockets.

He was not going to pick up that potato, and he was not going to pick up anything else either!

That evening, Mrs. Russet and Reid and Violet sat squished together at one end of the couch as they watched TV. The potato had a whole cushion to itself. Mr. Russet sat in the armchair, glowering.

HURON PUBLIC LIBRARY
521 DAKOTA AVE S
HURON, SD 57350-2797

As Mr. Russet continued his potato protest, the mess around the potato grew and grew and grew. One evening, Mrs. Russet reached under a couch cushion for the TV remote and ended up with a toothbrush and then a dirty sock and then an umbrella. Eventually, Violet found the remote in a soccer shoe under the dog bed.

HURON PUBLIC LIBRARY
521 DAKOTA AVE S
HURON, SD 57350-2797

FRISKY

Mr. Russet started spending a lot of time in potato-free rooms.

After five days, Mr. Russet's hairbrush got lost in the mess, and he stopped brushing his hair. After seven days, all of his coffee mugs also disappeared, and he started drinking his coffee out of soup bowls. After nine days, Mr. Russet noticed that the potato was wearing his favorite sunglasses, and he decided that he could take it no longer.

He picked up the potato.

That night, he prepared a mouthwatering feast for his family. There were hamburgers AND tacos AND noodles. And in the very middle of the table, Mr. Russet placed a steaming hot plate of golden french fries.

Mrs. Russet, Reid and Violet all smiled and reached for a delicious, crispy fry. And then, all at once, they stopped.

Violet looked at Reid, and Reid looked at Mrs. Russet, and Mrs. Russet looked at Mr. Russet. Then, ever so slowly, they leaned back in their chairs and peered into the living room.

Suddenly, no one was hungry anymore.

Well, almost no one ...

For my two little potato farmers, Robert and Ole, who inspired this story with their antics! — K.L.S.

For my dad, who cooks for our family. And my mom, who encourages me, and keeps me off the couch. — Y.H.

Text © 2019 Kerry Lyn Sparrow
Illustrations © 2019 Yinfan Huang

All rights reserved. No part of this publication may be reproduced, stored in a retrieval system or transmitted, in any form or by any means, without the prior written permission of Kids Can Press Ltd. or, in case of photocopying or other reprographic copying, a license from The Canadian Copyright Licensing Agency (Access Copyright). For an Access Copyright license, visit www.accesscopyright.ca or call toll free to 1-800-893-5777.

Kids Can Press gratefully acknowledges the financial support of the Government of Ontario, through Ontario Creates; the Ontario Arts Council; the Canada Council for the Arts; and the Government of Canada for our publishing activity.

Published in Canada and the U.S. by Kids Can Press Ltd.
25 Dockside Drive, Toronto, ON M5A 0B5

Kids Can Press is a Corus Entertainment Inc. company

www.kidscanpress.com

The artwork in this book was rendered in colored pencils, gouache and watercolor, and assembled in Photoshop.
The text is set in Absent Grotesque.

Edited by Yasemin Uçar and Debbie Rogosin
Designed by Marie Bartholomew

Printed and bound in Malaysia in 3/2019 by Tien Wah Press (Pte.) Ltd.

CM 19 0 9 8 7 6 5 4 3 2 1

Library and Archives Canada Cataloguing in Publication

Sparrow, Kerry Lyn, author
The couch potato / Kerry Sparrow ; [illustrations by] Yinfan Huang.

ISBN 978-1-5253-0005-9 (hardcover)

I. Huang, Yinfan, illustrator II. Title.

PS8637.P374C68 2019   jC813'.6   C2018-906061-1